Depersonalised

Andrijana Bulic

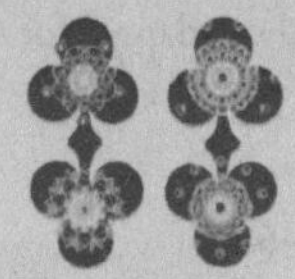

Four of Clubs Publishing

Print ISBN: 978-1-7643354-6-1

ePUB ISBN: 978-1-7643354-4-7

Published by Four of Clubs, Sydney, Australia.

Email: info.fourclubs@gmail.com

The depths that once haunted me,
have now become my solace.

DIS

BBBBBRRRRRRrrrrrrrrrRRRR-RRRRrrrrrrrrRRRRRRRRrrrrrrRR-RRRRR

The phone rang.

Shit. Fuck. You need to pick it up, Maddie! But I don't know what to say. You have to pick it up, it's your job. Fuck, why did I take this job?!

BRRRRRRrrrrrrrrrRRRRRRRRRBR-RRRRRrrrrrrrrrRRRRRRRR

Still ringing.

Okay. Three, two, one. Pick it up.

She forced the smile into her voice. "Superb Cleaning Solutions, this is Maddison speaking."

"Hey, p..t m..**e th**..ro...ugh to Cr..*ai*..g."

What did she say? I can't hear her.

"I'm sorry, I didn't quite get that. Could you please repeat?"

"Pu...t m..e thro...ugh to Cra..ig," the voice came again, this time more stern.

Did she say Craig? Gosh, my heart is pounding.

"Ummm, Craig? Can I ask who is calling?"

"It's StEp....h...S W..fe...."

"Umm, sorry, what was that?"

FUCCCK! I can't hear her.

"SttEp,,,h p..U..t mE thrOugh."

"Umm, Craig was it?" She put her hand on her head.

"P..**U**..*t m*E thr**O**ugh..."

A long awkward pause.

I can't hear her! Oh my God, Maddie! You can't ask her again... how embarrassing. Just put her through!

"Sure, I'll put you right through." She forced a smile through the phone.

No reply, just a deeply annoyed sigh.

Craig is the fucking boss. What if it was a scam caller and he comes down and yells at me? Fuck. What the fuck's wrong with you, Maddie? You're so bad at this. No, no, no! Don't fucking cry. Hold it in. Hold it in.

She held back tears and wiped her cheek, shuffling through the notes the receptionist-on-leave had left behind, trying to decipher admin she'd barely been trained for. She stared at the phone.

Please don't ring. Please don't ring.

BRRRRRRrrrrrrrrrRRRRRRRRRRRrrr-rrrrrRRRRRRRRRR

She jolted, heart thudding against her ribs.

Pick it up, don't think, Maddie. Just pick it up.

"Superb Cleaning Solutions, this is Maddison speaking."

"It's me, Raj. Can you come upstairs? Need to talk to you."

"Oh, okay... I'll be right there."

The office was a converted house, with payroll and reception downstairs and the CEO, Craig, and his managers upstairs. Raj, one of the man-agers, had hired her.

The interview had been... something. He asked about her experience, why she kept changing jobs so often, and why she didn't have a stable career. He went on about how, at her age, he was already married with two kids and had bought his first home.

Maddie had just sat there and offered the generic answers: she was passionate about growing with a company, and looking to get a foot in the door into admin, bla bla bla. She'd learnt through past experience to keep her ADHD and mental health struggles to herself, not to mention her excruciating endometriosis, the kind that made her bleed so heavily she could barely stand, sometimes passing out on the bathroom floor. People couldn't give a shit about that, especially men. To them, it just meant she was lazy, not trying hard enough. They'd always respond with some story about how they had even bigger struggles and still became successful.

It was only a two-week temporary job; the main receptionist was on holiday. She'd thought, *two weeks, I can survive that.*

Today was her second day. A nine-to-five in Gladesville. From Blacktown, she had to catch a train and two buses. She woke at 6:30, eyes barely open, and would go to bed at 11, then lie there until 3 a.m., her mind bursting with light and activity the moment she tried to switch off. She was exhausted but couldn't switch her mind off. Every possible scenario played on repeat, what she'd mess up, what she'd forget, how she'd look, what people would think. And that stupid phone sound ringing had already traumatised her.

Maddie knocked.

"Come in," he said, pointing to the chair in front of him.

She slipped inside and sat down. His face told her everything.

"So, Maddison," he began, passive-aggressive bullshit talk, "when you answer the phone, you need to be more switched on, yeah? That last call? That was Craig's wife." He paused, heavy with meaning.

Translation: *You stupid idiot. You're making me look bad. Do better!*

"Yes, Raj, it's just, you told me not to transfer calls straight to Craig, to always check who it was, so I was just being cautious."

"Yes, I understand that, but..." He let the pause hang, then leaned forward. "I hired you because I wanted to give you a chance. There were plenty of other qualified applicants, but I chose you." He pointed his finger at her.

Maddie clenched her fists under the desk, her pulse racing, her head spinning. *Don't talk to me like that.*

Raj kept going. "When you put the uniform on, I expect you to be professional, okay? You're not going to get far in life if you keep carrying on like this. You need to speak up. Be confident."

Her hands shook under the desk. She dug her thumb into her palm, the motion barely containing the trembling. Her mind screamed: *Say something! Tell him, he said it would be simple admin, just some paperwork at the back of the office, not fuckin' front desk! Minimal phones, just to get your foot in the door. Tell him you're on your own at reception, the other lady didn't explain shit. Tell him!*

But her mouth wouldn't open. She was frozen. Her body betrayed her.

"The job agency said you'd be a good fit," Raj went on. "Like I said, I'm giving you a chance because I saw potential in you."

Her teeth started chattering like she was standing in a freezer. Her body shook. And then, a sharp twitch, her leg kicking against the table. Raj jolted, startled.

"Are you... okay?"

"Aaah yeah...I'm just..."

Another twitch hit her, stronger this time. Her head jerked from side to side uncontrollably, and her whole body began shaking violently.

Fuck, Maddie! It's happening again! Stop! Stop! Not here, not now!

Raj just looked at her, eyes wide open in shock.

He's staring at me... how embarrassing!!!!!

A surge of energy shot up from the base of her spine to her head, like she was about to be blasted straight into the sky. Her heart pounded so hard it felt like it was about to burst. Her eyes rolled back in her head, and every nerve screamed.

No, no, no, no... Maddie, please stop! Please, not here!!

Then her vision split.

\\\\\\\\\\\\\\\\\\V///////////

She felt herself both in the office, sitting on the chair facing Raj, and simultaneously floating above her body on the right side, existing in two places at once.

Raj's expression turned from annoyed to worried. "Umm...".

Maddie's whole body was trembling. She clutched at her rib, trying to hold herself together, trying to control it, but she couldn't. She was slipping, swallowed by a black void, panic climbing up her throat. He was looking at her, but she couldn't recognise him; his face warped and he looked like a cartoon character. The whole room was now spinning, and she just felt like two eyes in a black void.

She jumped up, panic exploding through her.

"I... nEed... to gO."

She bolted out the door, down the stairs. The whole house spun. Her limbs felt gigantic, while her head felt tiny, like a grain of salt.

Complete diStortiOn.

She was hyperventilating, screaming inside her own head. She lunged toward reception, grabbed her bag, and stormed out of the building.

She ran out onto the street. The whole world felt weird, like a dream. She had no idea who she was, as if she were watching herself run frantically. She veered into a quiet side street, where she finally collapsed onto the pavement.

"It's okay, Maddie. Just breathe. Just breathe. You're okay." She rocked, head between her knees, the mantra spilling out between gasps.

"I'm gonna faint. It's happening, I'm gonna faint!"

She slapped her own face. 'No, you're not! You're pumped with adrenaline, you can't faint, she reassured herself. "Fainting comes from low blood pressure, but you're pumped with adrenaline. Your blood pressure is high. You can't pass out!"

Her hands fumbled through her bag. 'Smelling salts... get the smelling salts!"

The small aluminium fob clicked open. One sharp inhale, burning her nostrils, grounding her.

Earplugs. Put them on.

She shoved them in, shutting the world out. Silence. Only her breath remained.

Inhale. Exhale.

That's it.

You're okay.

Slowly, Maddie came back to herself.

She sat on the pavement, head between her knees, finally slowing her breath. And then it all came out.

"Why do you always fucking do this to yourself, Maddie!? I can't fucking do it! I CAN'T DO IT!!"

She wept openly, shoulders shaking. "I CAN'T DO IT!" She punched her chest. *What the fuck is happening to me?* She put her hands on her head.

Someone's gonna fucking see me...

She glanced around. The street was empty.

"So fucking embarrassing! Why am I like this? Why can't I be normal?"

Her tears still streaming.

Then **Brrrrbbbrrrrr.**

Her phone rang. It startled her. She looked. Sarah Job agency.

"Leave me the fuck alone!! "

She blocked the number, now yelling at her phone.

"F**U**ck Y**O**u! FU**uuuc**k Yo**U**!"

She closed her eyes and inhaled deeply, just sitting there for a moment.

"It's okay, Maddie... you'll get help. You'll get the help you need. Remember the comments on that reel... that therapy they talked about... EM something...You'll figure this out."

She got to her feet. Sliding on her sunglasses, she forced herself to walk, head down, towards the bus station. She put on her noise-cancelling headphones and turned on 432 Hz healing frequency music.

CON

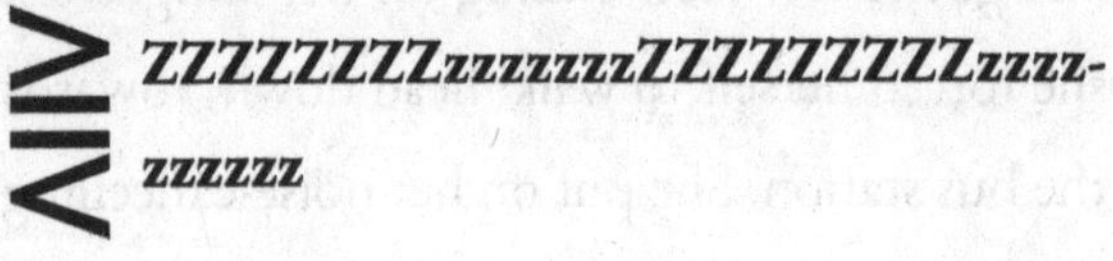

The white fluorescent lights buzzed and flickered overhead as Maddie sat in the waiting room, her leg bouncing uncontrollably, fingers drumming against her knee. She kept scanning the room, the receptionist on her right, a tatted bloke in a hat sitting in front of her, a mother with three kids to her left, trying to keep them in line.

"Sit down!" the mum snapped at one. "If you don't shut up, I'm puttin' wasabi sauce in ya mouth."

Maddie dropped her gaze, cheeks burning for no reason, her leg bouncing harder. She pulled her earplugs from her pocket, shoved them in. The noise dulled.

She grabbed her phone and checked her bank account.

$650.

Her stomach twisted.

$650. Half goes to Dad for rent. Which leaves me with what... a couple of therapy sessions at best? If I get the rebate... what was it called again...

"Maddison."

The doctor stood at the front of the waiting room, eyes scanning the crowd.

"Uh...yep." Maddie pushed herself up, legs stiff.

The doctor gave her a small smile, then turned. Maddie followed her down the corridor and into one of the rooms. She sat down while the doctor tapped away at her computer, eyes scanning the screen. After a moment, she turned.

"I haven't seen you in a while. How have you been?"

"Uh... yeah. I've been alright." *Just start with that intro, then tell her what you want.* She rubbed her thumb hard into her palm. "I actually wanted to..."

"I can see here that you haven't shown up to quite a few of your psychiatric appointments," the doctor interrupted.

Why is she looking at me like that? She's judging me...

"Are you taking your ADHD medication?"

"I... uh, actually wanted to talk to you about that..." Maddie cleared her throat, her thumb pressing harder into her palm, trying to steady herself. "I read online that there's a mental health plan that offers therapy for free, or at least at a lower price. Is that right?"

"Well, yes," the doctor said. "There is a mental health plan where you can claim up to ten subsidised sessions, depending on your condition."

Maddie's eyes lit up a little. "Okay... well, I'm interested in that. How do I get it?"

Her expression changed. Why did she do that face?

"Well, Maddison... sure, that sounds like a good idea, but what's going on with your medication? Have you stopped taking it?"

Shit. How do I tell... Fuck... my face is red. Now she's looking at me weirdly.

"Umm... I've actually stopped for a while because I just feel... I feel like it's not helping me anymore... like there's something..."

"Okay, well, that's not a problem," the doctor interrupted, typing rapidly at her keyboard. "We can look at adjusting your dose. I'll just make a note for your psychiatrist to review. Let's see... oh wow," she said, glancing at the screen, "your last appointment was six months ago."

"I actually..." Maddie interrupted, her voice shaky. "I actually want to try the therapy because I feel it could help me a lot. I... I researched a therapy called EMDR, which I think can help my nervous system..."

"Sure," the doctor cut in, still typing. "Once your psychiatrist adjusts your dose, we can set up the mental health plan."

"I... I just want to try the therapy first and see how that goes," Maddie said.

Fuck, the room feels weird again.

"Like I said, once you get your meds adjusted, we can definitely set that plan for you," the doctor said.

Why is she not listening to me?

Maddie's hands tightened in her lap.

I've been going to that psychiatrist for years, and it's only getting worse. And why does the fucking room feel so weird?

"I... I know, but I just really want to try the therapy first," Maddie said, her voice soft but tinged with annoyance.

The doctor forced a smile and paused for a moment. Then she turned to the printer and handed a piece of paper to Maddie.

"Give this to your psychiatrist," she said. "I've written down everything he needs to know.

Then come back here, and we'll set up your mental health plan, alright?"

Maddie took the paper, forced a small smile, and said quickly, "Ok, thank you." Then she left the room.

Fucking hell, she muttered to herself as she walked out of the practice. *Why can't she just give me what I want?* She wiped a tear. *I don't want to take your fucking medication anymore. Why can't anyone help me? So fucking tired of this shit.*

She walked to her car, got in, and slammed the door. Turned the engine on. Checked the petrol, almost empty. Pulled out her phone and checked her bank account again.

"Half goes to rent", she repeated out loud. "Fifty bucks for petrol, and I guess I can afford one therapy session... like 200 fucking dollars. Who can afford that shit?"

"Why don't you just take the meds, Maddie? Just do what they want…Cause I don't wanna fucking do what they want anymore. I'm obviously traumatised from something and I need therapy to figure it out!"

She sat in her beat-up car, clothes thrown over the seats, a mess all around her. She looked at her hands again.

"Why do I feel so numb? Fuck. I need to eat something… I'm feeling weird again. "

Buzzzzzzzzz.

Her phone vibrated on the seat beside her. She picked it up.

A message from Mum: *"Get a box of beer on your way home, you know which one your dad likes. I'll transfer the money."*

Maddie rolled her eyes.

She put her hand on the wheel and drove out of
the car park.

NEC

Maddie pulled up to her driveway and froze. Her dad's ute was parked out front, along with a few others.

Fuck... he's home early today, she sighed.

The garage was open. She knew exactly what that meant.

She quickly reparked her car on the street, ducked her head, and hurried out. Head down, she slipped through the front door, trying not to be seen. She grabbed a few things from the kitchen and headed straight to her room. Music blasted from the garage, mingled with loud laughter.

Her mum knocked on the door and poked her head in. "A few of your dad's mates are here to work on the retaining wall. Okay?"

Maddie didn't even look up from her phone. "Alright..."

"We're making a barbie for them," her mum continued. "Did you get the beer?"

"Yeah..."

"Okay, great," her mum said enthusiastically. "I'll save you some lamb chops for dinner."

And with that, she left the room abruptly.

Maddie sighed and threw herself onto the bed, exhausted. *So fucking noisy.* She shoved in her earplugs and tried to get some sleep.

About half an hour passed before she was jolted awake by loud yelling.

"You fucking liar!" "Hey! Hey! Hey!"

The muffled sounds came from outside.

What the fuck's going on?

Her chest tightened as panic began to rise. She got out of bed and walked toward the hallway, the yelling growing louder with every step. Through the window to the backyard, her eyes widened in disbelief. Her father and one of his friends were face-to-face, yelling at each other, the other men trying to hold them back. Her mother stood nearby, frozen, her face pale as she tried to calm her husband.

"Listen, mate! I don't care about the money, but you said you were gonna pay me! You lied to me!"

Her father's face was flushed, his words slurred, his body barely holding itself upright.

"Get fucked! You come into my house, I make you a BBQ, give you beers, and now you want money? Nah, mate, you're fucking wrong!"

He swung to punch him but missed completely, stumbling forward and crashing onto the ground.

"Duncan!" her mother screamed, rushing to his side.

Maddie ran out the back door, her heart pounding. "Dad! What's going on!?"

"Your dad's a liar!" his friend said.

He looked over to him and said, "Mate, don't ever call me again. I'm fucking done with you. You bastard."

And he walked away.

"Fuck yoooou!" her dad yelled from the ground.

"Listen, Duncan, I'm goin'. This is too much for me, mate," his other friend said.

"What's wrong with you!" Maddie yelled.

"You shut up!" her father yelled back. "I didn't do nothin'! That bastard comes into my house, drinks my beer, eats my food, and has the nerve to ask for money."

"But why are you so pissed? Look at yourself!" Maddie said, her face frowning.

Her father now slowly tried to get up. He shoved her mother's hands off him. "Get away from me!"

"Hey! Don't treat her like that!"

"You sh...U...t u...p!" he slurred his words. "Where's my fucking rent money, huh? Fucking disgrace you are." He spat to the side.

Maddie's heart started to beat faster. She took a step back as he approached her.

"You should be grateful that I'm letting you live here! You're almost thirty years old and look at you, fucking loser!"

"Duncan!" her mother interrupted.

"SHUT UP!!!" he turned to her, then continued, "You know how embarrassing it is when people ask about you? My grown, unmarried, childless daughter living with me. Look at your brother, has his own plumbing business, married with two kids. I knew you were gonna be a problem. Your fucking mother couldn't give me another son. You women are useless."

"This is Mum's house too!" Maddie fought back.

"I pay for everything!" He pointed a finger. "You think her shitty little pay does anything?"

"Mum told me I could stay! You know I have problems with anxiety and ADHD!"

"Aaah, fuck off with those excuses! You're making that all up in ya head. You're lazy, you're a bludger! I told you, if you don't find a job by the end of the month, you're out!

"Why can't you ever just understand me!?" Maddie's eyes filled with emotion now.

"Understand you? I've been way too understanding with you. When you were in primary school and they told us you had problems paying attention, I was understanding, so we put you on medication. But even then, you still didn't pay attention, cause you're lazy! And that's your problem! No pill's gonna fix that."

Maddie, now visibly shaking, stared at his face, it started to look distorted.

"But what do you expect from women?" he slurred. "Useless, weak, always a mess…"

"You kicked me out when I was eighteen! You didn't even give me a chance! I had to go work, pay rent, I couldn't even go to uni, how exhausted and broke I was!"

"Excuses again…"

Her mum approached. "Maddie, just leave him alone."

"NO!" she yelled, looking straight at her father. "You're a fucking drunk!"

He approached her, furious. "Don't you fucking speak to me like that!" He grabbed one of the chairs and threw it beside her.

"It's the truth! You're a lousy drunk, and that's all you'll ever be!

Get outta my house!!" His face was burning with rage.

She looked him dead in the eyes. "I don't need you, and I never did. You were never a father to me, you were just a provider. There's no differ-ence between you and the fucking dole, at least they didn't psychologically damage me."

She turned and left.

"How fucking dare you!" he yelled, kicking the table over.

Her mother tried to calm him. "Duncan, please, just leave her!"

Maddie rushed to her room and packed her bag quickly, her father still yelling from the back-yard, her hands shaking and heart pounding.

"Get outta my house!!"

She stormed out the front door and ran to her car, turning it on as fast as she could. She drove away, hyperventilating.

"Fuck, fuck, fuck..." Her head was spinning, her body shivering like she was freezing, barely able to keep the steering wheel steady.

Her vision blurred, and that weird split sensa-tion hit her again.

"nO, no, **No**, nO, n_o_..."

She gripped the wheel tighter.

"It's okay. You're okay, Maddie. Just breathe. Just..."

Her voice cracked.

"What if I fucked up? What if this is the end? What if I never come back?"

She quickly pulled over to the side of the road, far enough from her house.

"Fuck, I'm losing my mind... Come back, please, come back..."

Her chest tightened as she scrambled through her bag, hands shaking uncontrollably. "Where are they, where are they?"

She ripped open the bottle of anxiety pills. Empty.

"No**Oo***Oo***O**o! Why did you stop taking them, Ma**D**di*E*ee!"

She felt that deep, dark void wash over her again, like time had stretched into an endless expanse. Everything felt huge and unreal, the sensation was so uncomfortable she couldn't sense yesterday or tomorrow, just one infinite, unbroken stretch of now.

"Aaaa please not again. Distract yourself! 1, 2... **3,** 4, **5,** 6, 7, 8, **9**..."

She looked into the glovebox desperately trying to find some medication.

Nothing.

Looked under the seats.

Nothing.

"BLue duck... fYying in wAter... eAting piZ-za..." she muttered, voice trembling.

"1, **2,** 3, **4,** **5,** 6, 7... l**a** La **_la_** la l**A**..."

She found some old ibuprofen in a jacket in the backseat. She popped two into her mouth with shaking hands.

"Please help..." she whispered, barely audible.

"Please... somebody help me..."

TED

"I'm a bit scared to share this with you," Maddie said, her voice low.

"This is a safe space, and if you don't feel comfortable sharing, that's okay."

"It's just..." Maddie hesitated, rubbing her thumb into her palm. "I've been having this weird thing happen to me. It's gonna sound crazy, but... at times I feel like I'm not real. Like I'm watching myself in third person, and then everything feels fake, like it's all a dream."

"Mmm-hmm."

"And when it gets really bad," Maddie continued, "I feel like I'm split in two. Like I'm in my body but also outside of it. I can *feel* my presence outside of myself, and it just freaks me out. I haven't been able to return to myself... to feel normal."

She pressed her thumb harder into her hand. "I dunno. Maybe I've lost it and I just have to accept it."

The therapist leaned forward slightly. "And when this happens, what do people look like?"

"What do you mean?" Maddie asked.

"Do you recognise your friends and family, or not?"

"Well... when it's really bad, they look weird. Like, I *know* that's my mum, but it doesn't *feel* like her. I feel really numb."

The therapist asked, "And when does this usually happen?

Maddie paused, thinking. "Well... it happened when I was working this new job last week. It was really bad, I ran out of the manager's office and never came back."

"What happened there?"

"Well... he was judging me, telling me I wasn't doing a good job."

"Were you feeling anxious?"

"Yes, very," Maddie admitted. "I hate confrontations. I struggle to communicate with people because of my anxiety, it's like my brain works too fast and the words don't come out right."

"Mhmm," the therapist said, writing in her notebook.

Maddie continued, "And then... well, I got into a fight with my dad, and it was pretty bad. I moved back home a few months ago when I lost my job in retail. I really didn't want to go back, but I had no other option. I don't get along with my dad, he kicked me out after that fight, and I've been sleeping in my car for the past few days."

"Oh, okay...Do you have anyone you can stay with?"

"I usually crash at my friend's house, but I lost all my friends this year. I... I stopped talking to them."

"Why is that?"

"I dunno," Maddie shrugged. "My mental health got really bad, and I was struggling with money. Some of my friends got married, and everything was great for them, but I was just broken and depressed. It felt like our paths split. They said I was 'negative.' I was there for them at their lowest… and when I needed them, they weren't there."

"What about family? Do you have siblings who can help you?"

"I have a brother, but we don't really get along. He just had another baby, so I don't want to be a burden. Plus, if my dad found out, he would kick me out of that house too."

She sat, looking through the office window at the pedestrians walking by. "I have an aunt, my dad's sister, but I haven't spoken to her in years. She's a lawyer and lives in the city. She and my dad had a really big fight a few years back, and she distanced herself from the family."

"Maybe you could reach out to her. That support could really help you."

"Yeah, maybe... but I don't want to bother her."

"Maybe she's been wanting to reach out too," the therapist suggested gently, "but feels the same, not wanting to bother you. You both had a fight with your father... you have that in common."

Maddie sighed. "I guess I could try. I do miss her."

The therapist nodded, fidgeting with her pen. "So... tell me. What happened that day when you fought with your father? Did this feeling of *I don't feel real* happen then?"

"Yeah," Maddie whispered. "It was the worst then, and it scared me so much. I thought I was dying. I entered this... like this darkness, this void. It felt like I was having a psychotic break."

A pause hung in the room as the therapist wrote notes, the pen moving steadily across the page.

"I sound crazy, I know," Maddie said, fidgeting in her seat. "Maybe I'm just making all this up in my head."

"Listen, Maddie," the therapist said softly, offering a reassuring smile. "What's happening to you is actually okay. You're not going crazy, alright? It's what we call *dissociative anxiety*, or more commonly, *DPDR*, depersonalisation and derealisation. As crazy as it may feel, it's simply a symptom of anxiety. It's a protective mechanism. When your nervous system feels completely overwhelmed, it checks out, dissociates from the situation, to protect itself."

She grabbed her notebook and drew a straight line. "You see, there's a spectrum of dissociation. On the lower end, everyone experiences it; we daydream, or drive home and realise we weren't even aware of the drive, we zone out when someone is talking, or when we feel bored. This is mild, and everyone does it; it's our brain's way of escaping the present for a moment. But when it starts to move toward the middle of the spectrum, it can become quite uncomfortable. We begin to depersonalise, detach from our bodies, lose our sense of self, feel numb, and it's like watching yourself in a movie. Reality starts to feel fake, dreamlike. This usually happens after traumatic events or can be drug-induced, and there's often always a trigger.

She looked at Maddie, noticing her posture relax just a little. Then she drew a circle in the centre of her notebook, scribbling around it like a tangled spiderweb.

Because the experience feels so intense, many people start developing obsessive fears about it. They avoid situations or people that might trigger the state, becoming terrified of the DPDR itself. But DPDR isn't the real problem; it's a symptom of something deeper. It's the brain's way of saying, *'Hey, your nervous system is over-*

loaded. You've been pushing too hard for too long. You need to slow down.' When the brain notices that you're not taking steps to regulate, it steps in and tries to protect you. And it can create some of the most incredible illusions: some people feel like they're floating outside their bodies, others say their limbs feel distorted. Some even report auditory distortions or hallucinations. As frightening as it feels, this is actually one of the most primitive anxiety responses the brain has, like an emergency button that kicks in to keep you functioning when everything becomes too overwhelming.

"But why don't I feel like myself anymore?" Maddie asked quietly. "It's like the person I was is gone... and I feel like a stranger in my own body. Why can I come back to myself?"

"Well," the therapist said, "you've been bombarded with really intense situations, all happening in such a short amount of time. Your body's been in literal chaos, stuck in survival mode. And your mind is trying to cope the only way it knows how… by disconnecting."

Maddie sat in silence, contemplating her words, still rubbing her thumb against her hand. She stared at the notebook.

The therapist noticed Maddie's worried look. "DPDR is like a chronic daydream. People who experience it are usually quite imaginative and emotionally sensitive. They tend to feel more and have a rich inner world." She smiled. "There's a visual artist who sees me, and she experiences DPDR, but she doesn't call it that. To her, it's a strength. She says she detaches from her body, goes to a whole different place in her mind, and just paints. When she exits the trance, she's astonished by what she created, because she doesn't even remember painting it."

She looked at Maddie and smiled. "So, it's okay... It's safe to experience that state. You will always come back to yourself."

Maddie sighed, her shoulders relaxing just a bit.

The therapist said, "Put your hands on your heart and affirm with me: *I am safe in this feeling.*"

"I am... safe in this feeling..." Maddie muttered the words slowly. Then she kept repeating, "I am safe in this feeling. I am safe in this feeling..."

"Good," the therapist said, smiling warmly. "Your mind isn't broken, Maddie. It's just trying to protect you. The root cause is trauma, and unless we address it, we're only putting a band-aid over the symptoms. You see, most of what shapes us happens early on; those first five years of life lay the foundation for everything that follows."

Maddie held back tears. "I'm just tired... and I don't know what to do anymore. I can only afford this one session. I tried getting the mental health plan from my GP, but she wants me to go on medication again, which I really don't want to do... but I feel like I have no option."

The therapist leaned forward gently. "Maddie, I want you to know that I'm a registered therapist with the Hope & Safety Victims Recovery Scheme. It offers twenty-five free therapy sessions to victims of domestic violence. Have you ever witnessed or experienced any form of domestic violence?"

"No, no... I was never abused or anything like that," Maddie said quickly, brushing it off.

"It doesn't have to mean physical abuse," the therapist continued softly. "If you were yelled at, threatened, or even just witnessed violence in your home, if you lived in that environment, that's enough. You'd qualify for the sessions."

Maddie paused. "I mean... My dad's an alcoholic. He used to yell a lot when I was a kid, throw things, slam doors, and punch walls."

"Mmm," the therapist murmured, nodding slowly. "Then you've been a victim of his violence."

"No, no... he never hit us," Maddie insisted. "He'd just yell and get aggressive, put us in our place. We weren't allowed to talk back. I mean... It's his house. He pays for everything. Without him, we'd starve. That's what he always said, so he can do whatever he wants, right?"

The therapist met her gaze, steady and firm.

"No, he can't do whatever he wants, Maddison. That's emotional abuse. Providing for you doesn't give him the right to control or intimidate you. Just because he never hit you doesn't mean he didn't harm you. He wounded you emotionally, and your body remembers. It's screaming for you to heal the scars he left inside."

"Well, to me that's normal," Maddie said quietly. "And even though I know you're right, I still feel like he can do whatever he wants in his own home. Because at the end of the day, the one who has more money wins, and we either have to leave or accept his ways."

"An employer provides for their employees, right?" the therapist asked gently. "Does that give them the right to yell at them? To intimidate or terrorise them in the workplace?"

"No... that's not allowed," Maddie muttered.

The therapist nodded. "So why do you think it's alright for a father to do that to his own family? A home should be a place of safety, love, and comfort. If we don't feel safe in our own home, how can we ever feel safe outside of it?"

"Well, I don't know what safe even means," Maddie murmured. "My dad kicked me out the moment I turned eighteen. Said I was old enough to fend for myself, and if I couldn't, that was my problem."

"You may have left that house physically when you were eighteen, but emotionally, you're still there, still living under his control."

Maddie sighed. "If I apply for this domestic violence thing, are they gonna contact him? Or is he gonna get in trouble? I don't want that... I just want to heal."

"Nothing will happen to him," the therapist said reassuringly. "You're not filing a police report. You're simply naming him as the person who inflicted the violence on you. This is completely about you and your healing. Taking that first step is brave, it's admitting to yourself that you are a victim of domestic violence, and we can begin to heal all that trauma."

She paused, still rubbing her thumb against her palm. "I would really like that, to be able to understand where all these feelings come from and what they mean."

The therapist smiled gently and pulled out a thin horizontal LED light, placing it in front of her. "Do you know anything about EMDR?"

Maddie shook her head slightly. "A little... I read that some people said it really helped them heal trauma, but I don't really understand how it works."

The therapist nodded. "That's fine. I'll give you a brief explanation." She handed Maddie two small devices, one for each hand.

"It's called Eye Movement Desensitisation and Reprocessing. The light will move from left to right, and each device you're holding will gently vibrate as the light moves. This bilateral stimulation helps your conscious mind relax, which can often block or repress painful memories. The bilateral movement allows your subconscious to process these memories safely, releasing the emotional intensity and bringing clarity. We pick a topic to work on, you focus on the light, and we process whatever comes up."

She grabbed her notebook and drew a few circles. "We all have parts of ourselves that are disconnected. EMDR helps bring them back to the present, integrating them with your current self."

Maddie asked, "So you're saying that this thing that's happening to me, this dissociation, is because of trauma? I don't really get it, because yeah, I've been through a lot lately. I lost my job, I moved back home. But before in the past, I've been through worse things. Why didn't I have DPDR back then?"

The therapist nodded. "Well, because you might have reached your breaking point. There's only so much the mind can handle. Moving back home might have triggered it all, being back in your old room, hearing your parents talk, the scent of the house... something was triggered through the senses. And it seems, something within you wants to come through to be processed and healed. In other words, you might simply be ready to address these inner wounds."

Maddie stared at the LED light in front of her. "So... do I just think about something and look at the light?"

The therapist nodded. "Yes. And whatever comes up, we process it, then look at the light again and just keep processing."

"Okay... I'm a bit nervous."

"Just relax," the therapist said. "Take a deep breath in... and out. If at any time it becomes too much," she added, "you just let me know and we can stop at any time."

Maddie closed her eyes and took a deep, steady-
ing breath, letting it out slowly. She opened her
eyes and fixed them on the light in front of her.

"I'm ready."

I am

www.ingramcontent.com/pod-product-compliance
Lightning Source LLC
Chambersburg PA
CBHW012019110726
47994CB00009B/3231